Belinda 🐾 AND THE 🐾 Bears
and the
Porridge Project

Belinda 🐾 Bears
and the
Porridge Project

Kaye Umansky

Illustrated by
Chris Jevons

Orion
Children's Books

First published in Great Britain in 2015
by Orion Children's Books
an imprint of Hachette
Children's Group,
a division of Hodder and Stoughton Ltd.
Orion House
5 Upper St Martin's Lane
London WC2H 9EA
An Hachette UK company

1 3 5 7 9 10 8 6 4 2

The Orion Publishing Group's policy is to use papers that
are natural, renewable and recyclable products and made
from wood grown in sustainable forests. The logging and
manufacturing processes are expected to conform to the
environmental regulations of the country of origin.

A catalogue record for this book is available
from the British Library.

ISBN 978 1 4440 1349 8

Printed and bound in China

www.orionbooks.co.uk

For Freya, Elinor and Reuben

Contents

Chapter One

There were two cottages in Honeybear Lane. One had a door painted green. Behind that door lived Belinda, with her mum, dad and a cat called Gertie.

The second cottage was empty. Weeds grew in the garden. Brown paint peeled from the door. A 'FOR SALE' sign stood by the gate.

Belinda loved living in Honeybear Lane, but she wished they had neighbours.

One sunny afternoon, Belinda was walking home when she noticed a big change. The sign had gone. Curtains hung in the windows. The door had been painted blue.

Everything was lovely, except . . .
there was thick black smoke coming
from the kitchen window!

Belinda pushed open the gate
and ran up the path. She couldn't
see a bell or a knocker on the door.
Just a sign, which said:

PRIVATE!
LITTLE GIRLS
NOT WELCOME.

But this was an emergency!
Belinda banged on the door with
her fist.

"Hello?" she shouted.
"Is anyone in?"

There came the sound of footsteps.
A gruff voice said, "Who's that?"
"It's Belinda," said Belinda.
"I think there's something burning
in your cottage."
"We know," said the voice.
"Mummy burned the porridge."

"Oh," said Belinda. "That's all right, then. I just thought I'd tell you. In case you hadn't noticed."

She heard whispering. Then –

"Are you a little girl?" asked the voice.

"Yes," said Belinda. "I am."

"Are you a *greedy* little girl?" said the voice.

"I don't think so," said Belinda. "Sometimes I have second helpings of cereal in the mornings."

There was more whispering.

"Do you *break* things?" asked the voice.

"Not on purpose," said Belinda.

More whispering.

"Is your hair yellow and curly?" asked the voice.

"No," said Belinda. What odd questions! "It's brown and straight."

"Just checking," said the voice.
"Of course, you could be telling fibs."

"Well, I'm not," said Belinda.
"Open the door and see for
yourself."

There was a very long pause.
Then, slowly, the door opened and
Belinda saw her new neighbours.

Oh!

Chapter Two

Three Bears stood in the doorway.
Daddy Bear, Mummy Bear and
Baby Bear! Belinda knew the story.
She was lost for words.

"Sorry about the sign, but we have to be careful. Won't you come in?"

"Thank you," said Belinda. "Just for a minute, then."

"We're a chair short, I'm afraid. We had three in our last place," said Mummy Bear.

Baby Bear gave a little sniff and wiped his eyes with his paw.

"Cheer up, son," said Daddy Bear. "At least we saved your cushion."

"Where was your last place?" asked Belinda.

"Deep in the woods", said Mummy Bear. "Lovely it was. Quiet. Peaceful."

"Until the diggers came," said
Daddy Bear. "They knocked it down
to build a motorway. That was
the last straw. Especially after the
business with You Know Who."

"Goldilocks," whispered Baby
Bear. "She was called Goldilocks."
"Sssh, Baby," said his mother.
"We're trying to forget."

"Why did you choose Honeybear Lane?" asked Belinda.

"Mum liked the name," said Daddy Bear. "She thought we'd find lots of bears living here. Are there?"

"Well – no," said Belinda. "I haven't seen any."

"So we're the only bears in the village?"

"Um – yes," said Belinda.

The Three Bears looked worried.

"People are nice around here," said Belinda. "I'm sure you'll be welcome."

"Hmm," said Daddy Bear. "We're not too good at mixing. We were happy in our old house. Nobody bothered us there. Except You Know Who."

"You mean Gol—" said Baby Bear, before Daddy Bear put his paw over his mouth.

"Well," said Belinda. She thought she'd better change the subject. "You've got this house looking good."

"It is, isn't it?" said Mummy Bear. "Would you like to see the kitchen? The smoke must have cleared by now."

Chapter Three

The kitchen was painted a cheerful yellow. There was a round wooden table with three stools and a small oven. A saucepan was soaking in the sink.

"I'd offer you some porridge, but we've run out," said Mummy Bear. "It's a bit of a worry."

"Don't worry!" said Belinda. "They sell porridge in the village shop."

The Bears looked at each other.

"I don't think we're quite ready to go shopping," Mummy Bear said. "Not yet."

"How did you get your porridge when you were living in the woods?" asked Belinda.

"A farmer used to bring it on his cart," said Mummy Bear. "We usually get through a sack a week. And now we've used it all up."

"Don't know what we'll do for lunch," said Daddy Bear. "Or dinner. Or tomorrow's breakfast."

"You mean – you eat porridge every day? For every meal?" said Belinda.

"Of course," said Mummy Bear. "On Saturdays, we have it with honey – for a treat."

Belinda couldn't believe it. Porridge was nice, but not every day. Even with honey.

"Why don't you try something else?" she said. "For a change."

"Like what?" asked Daddy Bear.

"Cereal," said Belinda. "Or bread and butter, or cheese and apples, or vegetables … or homemade biscuits."

The Three Bears looked as if they had never heard of such strange things.

"What's homid bissits?" whispered Baby Bear.

Fancy not knowing about biscuits!
Belinda thought. Something had to
be done.

"Listen," she said. "I'm going
home now, but I'll be right back."

Chapter Four

Belinda's mum was in the garden when Belinda came running up the path.

"Hello, Mummy," said Belinda. "Can I have a picnic with The Three Bears?"

"Of course," said her mum, with a smile. Belinda was always making up stories. "Shall I pack a basket for you?"

"That's OK," said Belinda. "I'll do it."

In the kitchen, Belinda took the picnic basket down from the shelf and opened the cupboards.

Into the basket she put:

A carton of milk.   A packet of cornflakes.

A big wedge of cheese.   Three crusty bread rolls.

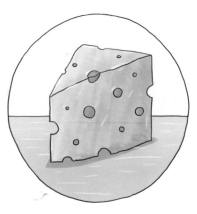
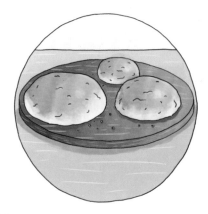

Three apples.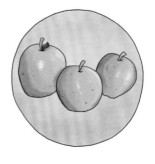

 A bunch of carrots.

A packet of flour.

 A packet of sugar.

A packet of butter.

For Belinda's last birthday, she had been given an apron, a chef's hat, a small rolling pin and some cookie cutters.

She popped those in too, closed
the lid, and set off back down the
lane.

Chapter Five

The Three Bears' eyes went wide
when they saw Belinda's heavy
picnic basket.

Daddy Bear carried it into the kitchen and put it on the table.

"Can I open it?" said Baby Bear. He was very excited. *"Peeze? Peeze?"*

Daddy Bear lifted him up and Baby Bear threw back the lid.

"What's all this?" said Daddy Bear.

"Food," said Belinda. "Different sorts. Not porridge."

"I don't know," said Daddy Bear. "We're used to porridge. We might not like it."

"You won't know unless you try," said Belinda. "That's what my mum always says. Shall we lay the table?"

"We've only got bowls and spoons," said Mummy Bear. "That's all you need for porridge."

"Those will do," said Belinda.

Daddy Bear and Mummy Bear
set out a big bowl, a medium bowl
and a tiny bowl.

Baby Bear unpacked the basket,
with excited squeals.

Belinda opened the cornflakes
and poured some into the bowls.
She added milk and sugar.

"That's it," said Belinda.
"Now you eat it."

Nobody moved.

"Go on," said Belinda. "Just try.
I thought bears were supposed to
be brave."

"I am," said Baby Bear suddenly.
"I'm brave." He dipped his spoon
into the bowl and had a tiny taste.

"Well, do you like it, Baby?" asked his parents.

"I do," said Baby Bear, dipping his spoon again. "It's just right.

Chapter Six

After that it was easy. The Bears
couldn't wait to try everything.
      The air was full of happy
crunching and munching noises.
Finally, everything was gone.
Even the apple cores!

"That was the best meal I have ever eaten," said Daddy Bear. "I didn't miss porridge at all, did you, Mum?"

"Not one bit," said Mummy Bear.

Baby Bear was too busy licking butter from his paws to talk.

"Now there's something else I want to do," said Belinda. She had saved the best until last.

"What is it?" asked Mummy Bear.

"We're going to make sugar biscuits," said Belinda.

So that's what they did.

Mummy Bear stirred (with help from Baby Bear).

Daddy Bear rolled the dough (with help from Baby Bear).

Baby Bear cut out the cookies
(with help from Belinda).

Then he licked the bowl, all by
himself.

When the biscuits came out of
the oven, they didn't last long!

"Did you have a nice time with the Bears?" asked Belinda's mum that night.

"Yes," said Belinda. "I taught them how to make biscuits."

"I bet they liked those," said her mum.

"They did," said Belinda.
"Tomorrow, I'm taking them an egg
so we can bake a cake. They were
worried about being the only bears
in the village, you see, but I think
they're feeling better now."

"You're being very helpful to those bears," said her mum.

"I am," said Belinda. "In fact, I don't know what they'd do without me."

MAKE YOUR OWN SUGAR BISCUITS!

Makes about 12 biscuits
50g sugar
50g butter
400g self-raising flour

1. Pre-heat the oven to 190C/375F/Gas 5
2. Mix the butter and sugar together until creamy, then slowly add the flour to make a dough.
3. Roll out the dough. Cut into shapes with a cookie cutter.
4. Lay your biscuit shapes on a baking sheet greased with butter, then bake for 12-15 minutes until golden.

What are you going to read next?

Have more adventures with Horrid Henry,

or save the day with Anthony Ant!

Become a superhero with Monstar,

float off to sea with Algy,